21st
Century
Skills Library

HEALTHY FOR LIFE

SNOWBOARDING

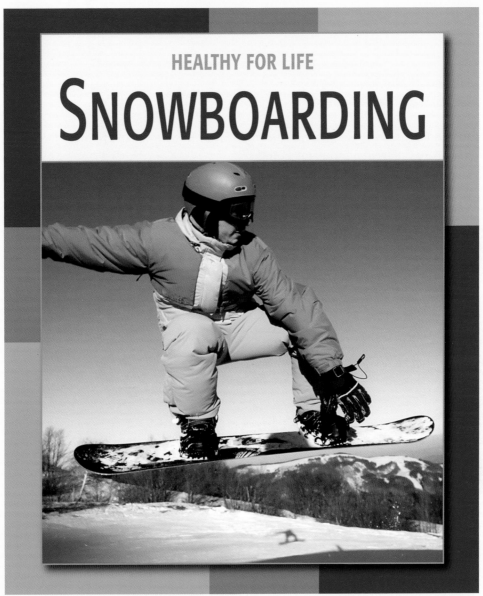

Jim Fitzpatrick

Cherry Lake Publishing
Ann Arbor, Michigan

Published in the United States of America by Cherry Lake Publishing
Ann Arbor, MI
www.cherrylakepublishing.com

Content Adviser: Thomas Sawyer, EdD, Professor of Recreation and Sports Management, Indiana State University, Terre Haute, Indiana

Photo Credits: Page 5, © Andrew P. Scott/Dallas Morning News/Corbis; page 7, AP Photo/Alden Pellett; page 9, © James Leynse/Corbis; page 20, © Jeff Curtes/Corbis; page 24, © Karl Weatherly/Corbis; page 25, © John Mabanglo/epa/Corbis; page 28, © Shawn Frederick/Corbis

Library of Congress Cataloging-in-Publication Data
Fitzpatrick, Jim, 1948–
  Snowboarding / by Jim Fitzpatrick.
    p. cm. — (Healthy for life)
  ISBN-13: 978-1-60279-018-6 (lib. bdg.)   978-1-60279-092-6 (pbk.)
  ISBN-10: 1-60279-018-3 (lib. bdg.)   1-60279-092-2 (pbk.)
  1. Snowboarding—Juvenile literature. I. Title. II. Series.
  GV857.S57F58 2008
  796.939—dc22   2007008348

*Cherry Lake Publishing would like to acknowledge the work of
The Partnership for 21st Century Skills.
Please visit* www.21stcenturyskills.org *for more information.*

TABLE of CONTENTS

CHAPTER ONE

HITTING THE SLOPES

Are you ready for some fun? Try snowboarding!

Snowboarding is one of the world's fastest-growing sports. Around the globe, people enjoy gliding down mountain slopes atop the powdery snow. In fact, snowboarding has become so popular that some snowboarders won't wait for winter to enjoy it. Today, there are more than 30 indoor snowboarding parks worldwide!

Only a few short years ago, many traditional ski resorts refused to allow snowboarding. People at the ski resorts thought snowboarding was dangerous. They believed all snowboarders were reckless and posed a danger to skiers. But over the years, snowboarding has become more acceptable, mainly because it has become so popular. Snowboarding has been acknowledged as a real sport—there are even snowboarding competitions in the Olympics. Teenage Olympic gold medalist Shaun White is greeted as a world-class athlete wherever he snowboards.

Snowboarder Shaun White won a gold medal in the men's halfpipe event at the 2006 Olympics.

The origins of snowboarding are closely tied to surfing and skateboarding. In the 1960s, a Michigan man named Sherman Popper connected two skis together. He called his invention the Snurfer, because it was a lot like surfing on snow. Kids loved the Snurfer, and in 1965 nearly a half million Snurfers were sold. By 1977, Tom Sims and Jake Burton Carpenter had created boards that are more like today's snowboards. At

The vast majority of snowboarders are in their teens or early twenties.

Jake Burton Carpenter was an early snowboard innovator.

How do people come up with new ideas? You can't buy originality or inventiveness, but there are strategies you can learn that will help you to be more creative. Tom Sims, Jake Burton Carpenter, and Chuck Barfoot were deeply involved in the sport of skateboarding. They wanted to enjoy their sport in the winter, so they dreamed up an innovative way to do that—by creating modern-day snowboarding. For these snowboarding pioneers, creativity was a matter of taking something old, changing it a bit, and turning it into something totally new.

the time, Sims was a champion skateboarder with his own skateboard company. One of his close friends, Chuck Barfoot, was also important in early skateboard and snowboard manufacturing. The snowboards made by these pioneers serve as the basis for the snowboards used today.

Life & Career Skills

There was a time when snowboarders were not welcome at ski resorts. For many years, resorts banned snowboarders from their slopes. Thankfully, in recent years, ski resorts and skiers have proved to be flexible and adaptable. They worked with snowboarders to maintain ski resorts and slopes. Skiers and snowboarders have learned to enjoy their sports together on the slopes.

These days, both sports feed off of the energy and excitement of the other. Skiers and snowboarders are influenced and inspired by one another, which helps spread the popularity of all winter sports. In a way, they have become each other's strongest ally.

An estimated four million people around the world are snowboarders. These days, most ski resorts allow snowboarders to ride alongside skiers. And many resorts now have areas called **snow parks**, which include **half-pipes** and jumps specifically designed for use by snowboarders and "extreme" skiers. There are even winter resorts dedicated solely to snowboarding.

Today's snowboarders know that nothing feels quite like snowboarding down a mountain on a slope of fresh **powder**. Imagine your feet attached to pillows that carry you downhill. That's a bit like how it feels to snowboard on freshly fallen snow. Once you've had the experience, you'll want to head back to the mountain again and again.

CHAPTER TWO

CHOOSING A BOARD AND MORE

Snowboarding is a young sport, and snowboards have come a long way in the past 40 years. Back when the sport was getting started, snowboards were not sleek and powerful. Sometimes, they consisted of little more than old wooden ironing boards with bicycle inner tubes wrapped around them to hold the rider's feet in place.

Snowboards come in many different sizes. All snowboarders can find boards that fit them perfectly.

Snowboards are made of wood covered with fiberglass and plastic.

Today's modern snowboards are high-tech marvels. The core of the snowboard is a piece of wood. The board is covered in a layer of fiberglass that is laminated, or sealed, in plastic. On the bottom of the snowboard is a layer of polyethylene, a kind of plastic. This is the slippery surface that slides along the snow. A strip of steel wraps around the edge of the board. The steel makes it easier for the rider to grip the snow and ice and make turns. Now, boards also have contoured noses and tails, which improve control and performance.

Many different types of snowboards are available. Some boards are good for speeding downhill, while others are better for doing jumps and other tricks. When choosing a snowboard, people also need to consider their body size and level of experience.

Most beginners start with short boards because they're the lightest and most maneuverable. This makes them the easiest to learn on. Short boards typically reach a rider's collar bone or chin. Medium-length boards reach the rider's chin or nose. Long boards reach the rider's eyes or top of head. They are the best for big mountains and high-speed snowboarding. Long boards are more stable but harder to maneuver. A board's width is determined by the size of the boarder's feet. The snowboard boot should extend just over the board's edge. If the board is too wide, it's hard to maintain control during turns.

The snowboard is only the first piece of equipment you'll need before you're ready to head out on a slope. Beginning snowboarders must decide which kind of bindings and boots they want. Bindings are used to attach the board to the boot. There are two basic types: step-in bindings and strap bindings. Step-in bindings are considered more convenient because you can put them on while standing up. You must sit down—often in the snow—to attach strap bindings. But strap bindings have their advantages. They are adjustable and used with softer, more comfortable boots. Step-in bindings require a stiffer boot.

Today's snowboarders can choose from dozens of different types of boots. Snowboarding boots are designed for comfort and safety. It is especially important that the boots support the foot and ankle in order to prevent injury.

Strap bindings are used with soft, flexible boots.

Snowboarders need specialized clothing to protect themselves from the sometimes brutal winter weather. They must be able to tolerate driving winds and temperatures below freezing. A good waterproof outer shell is a must. Beneath it, snowboarders need several layers of wool, silk, or fleece. Dressing in layers allows you to control your body temperature by adding or removing layers as conditions change.

Once fully equipped, snowboarders are ready to enjoy one of today's most exciting sports. But before you even go outside, familiarize yourself with your equipment. You can learn how to get on your board and practice attaching your bindings long before you go to the mountain.

Often, that first day on the slopes is tough. Many beginners find themselves baffled by even the most simple snowboarding moves. Just standing on a snowboard can be

21st Century Content

Snowboarding is a fun and healthy activity, but it can also be costly. Between resort fees, equipment, and even a hot chocolate in the ski lounge, a day of snowboarding can do some damage to your wallet. Snowboards start at about $100, snowboard boots cost between $50 and $200, bindings are another $50, and a good jacket is often more than $100.

Because the equipment is so expensive, it's important to think carefully before you buy anything. You should select equipment that will keep you safe, that you know you will use, and that will save you money.

If you only go snowboarding once or twice a year, renting equipment may be the right move for you. But if you plan to snowboard regularly, buying your own board and equipment may be a better idea. Analyze your needs, and make smart consumer choices before hitting the slopes.

Snowboarders are constantly innovating, pushing the limits of what anyone thought was possible. Modern snowboarding tricks are similar to those used in skateboarding and surfing. The most basic trick is the ollie, which revolutionized skateboarding before being applied to snowboarding. A skateboarder ollies by lifting the front foot while stomping the rear foot on the tail of the board, all while jumping into the air. If a skateboarder ollies successfully, the skateboard will pop off the ground beneath his or her feet.

A snowboarder ollies in the same way, though there is one big difference. The snowboard is attached to the rider's feet, so a snowboarder's ollie is easier because the snowboarder only has to jump up to get the board in the air. Today, skateboarders and snowboarders collaborate to develop exciting new tricks to perform in their sports. They share ideas and both take credit for the new maneuvers.

challenging for a beginner. One basic skill to develop is changing direction on the slope by switching edges from toe side to heel side. Skating—gliding with one foot in the bindings and the other pushing like a skateboarder—is important for knowing how to get on and off the lifts that take riders up a mountain.

Resorts and snowboard camps usually have instructors who can take most beginners from the basic skill level to an intermediate level within a few short hours. These same instructors often provide the lessons needed for intermediate snowboarders to learn tricks such as riding half-pipes. With a few tips from an instructor, a willingness to learn, and a lot of practice, beginners will be doing 180 alley-oops on the half-pipe before they know it!

CHAPTER THREE

SNOWBOARDING SAFETY

Snowboarding is fun but exhausting.

Snowboarding is tremendously popular, but it is also risky. One of the most important factors in snowboarding safety is overall fitness. A beginner watching intermediate- or advanced-level snowboarders riding down a slope may get the impression that it's easy. Although basic skills can be learned in a day, snowboarding requires an all-out physical effort. Its physical demands may exhaust beginners. In fact, fatigue is often a

Snowboarders face many dangers. Frostbite can occur when you spend a long day in the cold. To protect yourself, cover as much of your skin as possible. If any part of your body begins to feel numb, get back inside. An even more serious condition is hypothermia. This is an extreme drop in your body temperature. It is caused by being out in very cold temperatures or by being wet and cold. Hypothermia can be deadly, so knowing its early symptoms, such as shivering and chattering teeth, is vital. If someone has these symptoms, they should go inside right away. To prevent hypothermia, dress warmly, stay dry, and take breaks to warm up.

Common snowboarding injuries include bruises, cuts, sprains, fractures, and head traumas. It's important to know what to do in case of an accident. Before you head up the mountain, make sure that you know where the nearest first aid kit is. You should also know who to contact at the resort in case of an emergency. Remember, having fun is important, but safety is your priority!

factor in most snowboarding injuries. When people get tired, they don't think as clearly and their muscles can't react as quickly.

More than 90 percent of snowboarding injuries result from falls, mainly on hard-packed snow or ice. Falling is one way of stopping while snowboarding. Another way to stop is by using basic turns. It is important that beginners learn to control their boards so they can use this safer way of stopping.

Because falling is so common for beginners, it's important to wear safety equipment. When you fall, it's natural to put out a hand to catch yourself. If the snow is icy or firmly packed, this can easily lead to injury. Many snowboarders wear hand and wrist supports to protect themselves. The best way to protect your

*A good-fitting helmet will prevent head injuries
during most snowboarding falls.*

wrists is to learn how to fall properly. Keep your arms tucked in, and roll out of the fall.

Other injuries caused by falling include strains to the knees or ankles. Properly fitted boots and bindings can help prevent such injuries.

Among the most important pieces of safety equipment are a properly fitted helmet, which protects your head from falls, and UV- reducing

Members of the snow patrol tend to an injured snowboarder.

goggles, which shield your eyes from the dangerous rays of the sun. And
remember, wearing a helmet does not make a snowboarder invincible.
Most helmets will protect a snowboarder from a typical fall, even in
icy conditions. But a helmet cannot necessarily protect a snowboarder

traveling 25 to 35 miles per hour (50 to 60 kilometers per hour) who collides with a tree.

Conditions are also an important factor in snowboarding safety. It's crucial for riders to always be aware of snow and weather conditions. The weather can change quickly as storms race over the mountains. Winds and frigid temperatures affect the snow's surface, quickly transforming soft, powderlike snow into ice. Most resorts post weather conditions. Lift operators are often a good source of information about the weather at the top of the mountain, where the conditions can be radically different from those at the bottom of a **run**.

Snow patrols can help snowboarders when conditions change or if someone gets injured. But the best approach to safety while snowboarding is to know your limits and ride only on slopes and in conditions that

When you are snowboarding, you are responsible for your own safety. You have to assess your own abilities and make appropriate choices about what you should or should not try.

Most resorts have a number of different runs, typically identified by colors and images. These runs provide options from beginner's levels (often Green or Blue) to advanced levels (such as Black Diamond) that challenge the most accomplished boarders. Runs are evaluated on their steepness and width. Steeper and narrower runs are for more advanced riders.

Snowboarders must use this information to make good decisions that will keep them safe on the slopes. Snowboarding instructors will recommend which slopes or runs students should try. But there's no one at the top of the run who will evaluate a rider's ability. It's up to the individual snowboarder to make the right choice.

*Snowboarding is a great way to have fun
and enjoy some amazing scenery.*

you can handle. The logical approach is to start with the easiest runs. Make sure you can ride them before trying the more challenging runs. Often, snowboarders will discover that their abilities develop quickly over the span of a few days. So it isn't long before the more challenging and exciting runs become part of their everyday snowboarding experience!

CHAPTER FOUR

YOUR SNOWBOARDING ENVIRONMENT

Snowboarders need mountains. And not just any mountain will do. Snowboarders need the right kinds of slopes, the right kinds of weather, the right kinds of snow. Because snowboarders are always on the lookout for the best opportunity to ride, they become very aware of the natural world. This often results in a deep appreciation for the environment.

One of the great pleasures of snowboarding is being outside on a crisp, clear day.

Part of your responsibilities as a snowboarder is to be aware of your surroundings. You should do your part to help maintain your snowboarding environment. If you see litter on the slopes, pick it up and throw it away in the nearest trash can. Even if it is not your litter, you still have a responsibility to yourself and others to keep the slopes and trails clear of anything that could cause accidents. By being aware of environmental issues, and by doing your part to keep the slopes clean, you will ensure that others will be able to enjoy the mountains for year to come.

It's important to be a good environmental citizen when you're on the slopes. If a run is closed or a sign says to keep out of an area, there's usually a good reason. Perhaps the area has been closed to protect the plants and animals that live there. Snowboarders should also avoid riding through the trees. You may knock off branches or kill young plants that are growing under the snow.

Throw away any litter you find while snowboarding.
It's up to you to keep the slopes clean.

Heli-snowboarding gives boarders the chance to glide down fantastic, isolated slopes.

Today, many snowboarders find the resorts too crowded. So how do you truly get away from it all while also having an extraordinary snowboarding experience? Some try **heli-snowboarding**. Heli-snowboarding is an expensive alternative to taking a resort chairlift to the top of a mountain run. Instead, a helicopter transports the snowboarders to pristine mountain slopes covered with fresh powder.

Once snowboarders are deposited on an isolated mountain slope, they must rely upon their own judgment to find paths down through unknown terrain. This can be dangerous in areas prone to avalanches. A person swept away by a huge onrush of snow can die. Despite the risks, heli-snowboarding is growing in popularity. People want experiences no one else has enjoyed. They are looking for the ride of a lifetime.

Snowboarders left tracks in the snow after helicopters brought them to this mountain in Alaska.

Snowboarding takes balance, coordination, and quick thinking.

Did you ever wonder how many calories you burn swimming? How about brushing your teeth? Look at the chart below to see how many calories you burn doing different activities. This chart is for a person who weighs 100 pounds (45 kilograms). If you weigh more, you'll burn a little more. If you weigh less, you'll burn a little less.

Activity	Calories
Basketball	500
Running	450
Snowboarding	380
Dancing	300
Swimming	275
Riding a bike	250
Skateboarding	230
Brushing teeth	115
Watching TV	50

exhausting. But that workout only makes your body stronger for the next day's runs!

To glide smoothly down a snowy mountainside, snowboarders combine mind and body skills. Snowboarders must sometimes make split-second decisions. They must stay alert to avoid trees, rocks,

The best snowboarders have tremendous physical and mental skills.

and other riders. Quick turns and adjustments are essential to safe snowboarding.

Whether charging down a mountain run or doing complex tricks like that 180 alley-oop, snowboarding demands both mental and physical strength. It takes skill and courage. But it also provides great thrills for everyone who tries it. A snowboarder who gets beyond the basics will have discovered one of life's great joys!

21st Century Content

Snowboarding contests are popular all over the world. These events promote global awareness because people from many cultures and countries come together to share their love of snowboarding. Many types of snowboard contests have developed through the years. Today, formats include half-pipe, side-by-side downhill races, and Boarder X, in which as many as four competitors race down a course with jumps and gaps while trying to avoid collisions.

Snowboarding became an Olympic sport in 1998. Other big contests include the Gravity Games, ESPN's Winter X Games, and World Cup Snowboarding, which includes meets in the United States, Canada, Japan, and Europe. Many of these events are broadcast on television to the thrill of fans around the world.

Glossary

180 alley-oops (WON A-tee a-lee-OOPS) 180-degree turns in the air while going in an uphill direction

bindings (BYND-ingz) fasteners that connect the boots to the snowboard

half-pipes (HAF-pipes) U-shaped snow structures, similar to skateboarding ramps, for freestyle snowboarding

heli-snowboarding (HE-luh-SNO-bord-ing) a type of snowboarding in which helicopters transport snowboarders to remote mountain slopes

nose (NOZE) the front end of the snowboard

ollie (AH-lee) jumping into the air by lifting the front foot while stomping on the rear of the board

powder (PAU-dur) freshly fallen snow atop a firmer base of previously fallen snow

run (RUN) a course down a mountain slope

skating (SKAYT-ing) gliding on a snowboard with one foot in the bindings while the other foot pushes like a skateboarder does

snow park (SNO PARK) a special area in a resort that features jumps, railings, half-pipes, and other elements for snowboarders and skiers

tail (TALE) the back end of a snowboard

FOR MORE INFORMATION

Books

Gifford, Clive. *Snowboarding.* New York: DK Publishers, 2007.

Masoff, Joy. *Snowboard! Your Guide to Freeriding, Pipe & Park, Jibbing, Backcountry, Alpine, Bordercross, and More.* Washington, D.C.: National Geographic, 2002.

U.S. Olympic Committee. *A Basic Guide to Skiing and Snowboarding.* Torrance, CA: Griffin, 2002.

Woods, Bob. *Snowboarding.* Chanhassen, MN: Child's World, 2005.

Web Sites

ABC-of-Snowboarding
www.abc-of-snowboarding.com
A good source for information on equipment, skills, and safety

Snowboarding.com
www.snowboarding.com
To find all kinds of information about gear, resorts, and more

The United States of America Snowboard Association
www.usasa.org
A helpful resource for finding out more about contests and the best riders

INDEX

ABOUT THE AUTHOR

Jim Fitzpatrick has been involved with board sports since 1957. He was a long-time skateboarder and surfer by the time he first snowboarded in the 1980s. "It was a disaster!" he claims. Since then, he has become an accomplished snowboarder, and now he can't decide which board sport he enjoys the most. Once an editor for TransWorld Publications, he is currently a vice president of USA Skateboarding. A California native, Jim lives in Santa Barbara, where he is the head of the Santa Barbara Montessori School. Santa Barbara is a five-hour drive from Mammoth Mountain, but Jim makes sure that the school's junior high students spend part of their winter snowboarding!